KT-553-041

# CONTENTS

With countries in chaos and the world at war, Earth faced its darkest hour. To answer its cry for help, the Amazons on the secret island of Themyscira held a contest to find their strongest and bravest champion. From that contest one warrior – Princess Diana – triumphed over all and boldly entered the world of mortals. Now her mission is to conquer villainy, defend justice and restore peace across the globe.

She is . . .

# WONDER WOMAN

## ★ THE AMAZING AMAZON ★

# CHAPTER 1

## EVIL STIRS

Deep beneath the streets of London, the Servants of Evil marched through an underground crypt. They wore long, black cloaks with hoods, and stark white masks to hide their faces.

As minions of an unknown master, the Servants usually committed small crimes. But their meagre missions were about to be upgraded. The head of the organization, the Herald, had called them all to the main chamber for an important announcement.

The Servants anxiously filed into the fearsome chamber. The crypt was dark, and the air was damp. Flickering torches lined the walls. Iron chandeliers hung from the ceiling.

**BAM!** A large wooden door flung open, startling the assembled group.

"He comes!" one of the Servants of Evil cried out.

At last, the Herald came out of his private quarters. He was dressed in a blood-red cloak that hid his face. The crowd stirred with excitement, but one among them didn't share her feelings. Hidden among the Servants of Evil stood a hero in disguise – Wonder Woman.

The Amazon warrior had heard about the group's activities. After suspecting the group might be up to something evil, she had secretly invaded its ranks.

Donning the Servants' trademark black cloak and white mask, Wonder Woman had slipped into their underground headquarters unnoticed. Now, surrounded by enemies, she waited for the right time to strike.

The Herald gazed out at his followers bowing before him. "Greetings, Servants of Evil!" he exclaimed, his voice echoing through the chamber. "I bring good news to all of you. Our master is very pleased."

"All hail the master!" the group shouted together.

The Herald snapped his fingers. A faithful Servant brought forth a metal case. He opened it to reveal what looked like a gold sword handle with a ruby crystal at one end.

"We have recovered the item our master desires," said the Herald. He took it into his hands and held it high for all to see.

"Simple though this may look," the Herald continued, "many among us have paid a high price to find this precious relic. Let us give thanks to them as we remake the planet."

"But only after we destroy it!" another Servant cried out.

Wonder Woman had heard enough. She whipped off her cloak, revealing her true identity to the crowd.

"You won't be destroying anything today!" the hero shouted. "Whatever you're planning is officially *over*."

"How did *you* get in here?!" the Herald asked. "Nothing escapes my notice!"

"Serving your dark master has blinded you, Herald," the Amazon Princess replied. "I urge you to surrender peacefully."

Four more Servants charged Wonder Woman. She dropped to the ground and swept her leg across the floor, knocking them all off their feet. As they struggled to recover, more Servants closed in.

Wonder Woman had to act fast. She spotted six iron chandeliers hanging above the chamber. Each one was attached to the ceiling with thick, sturdy chains.

*These chandeliers will help me contain the Servants without hurting them,* Wonder Woman thought. She threw her tiara through the air like a boomerang. It ripped through the links of the chains in an instant. The iron chandeliers fell onto the Servants, trapping them tightly.

Wonder Woman spotted the gold handle and reached for her magic lasso.

"I'll be taking that!" the hero exclaimed.

Wonder Woman whipped her lasso. In a flash, the item flew out of the Herald's hands and into her own.

The Herald quickly ran to the corridor. The Amazon snagged his foot with her lasso and dragged him back into the chamber.

"You will not stop us," the Herald warned. "We serve a greater power. Our master will protect us. You'll see. You'll *all* see."

"Who is your master, and where can I find him?" Wonder Woman asked. "Tell me the truth." She looped her lasso around the Herald and focused its power.

The Herald shook his head. "I do not know. Our leader's identity is a mystery even to us," he said. "We simply follow orders."

Wonder Woman inspected the handle. "What is this?" she asked.

"Something our master has wanted for a very long time. We went to great lengths to find it, though we do not know what it does," said the Herald. "The master tells us it will change the course of history."

"Your master is lying to you," Wonder Woman said, attaching the sword handle to her belt. "I intend to find him and make him pay for his evil ways."

"Hahahahaha!" The Herald laughed as Wonder Woman released her lasso. "You're playing with forces you do not understand."

"I'm not afraid," Wonder Woman said, staring at the Herald. "I suggest you change your ways. I'll be watching," she warned. "Your master is about to learn his place."

Wonder Woman left the underground base and contacted the London police. They swiftly arrived and arrested the Servants.

With the sword handle safely in hand, Wonder Woman boarded her Invisible Jet. She fired up its engines and set out for the Museum of Natural History in Washington, DC. She hoped the museum's new curator, Professor Milton, would be able to shed some light on the mysterious object.

On the way, Wonder Woman realized she might need a helping hand on this mission. She sent her close friend Steve Trevor a message to meet her at the museum. Steve was a secret agent with the spy agency known as A.R.G.U.S.

When Wonder Woman arrived at the museum, she found Professor Milton in her office. Milton was a small woman with scraggy, blonde hair and thick, crooked glasses. She wore an oversized jumper and was focused on a jar of cookies in her hand.

"Oh my," Professor Milton gasped, surprised to find Wonder Woman standing there. "I wasn't expecting a guest!"

"I'm sorry, Professor Milton. I didn't mean to startle you," Wonder Woman said. "We haven't had a chance to meet. I am Diana of Themyscira."

"I know who you are, of course. The great Wonder Woman. It's a pleasure." Professor Milton chuckled. She placed the jar on her desk and straightened her glasses. "How can I help you today?"

Wonder Woman revealed the gold handle. "I need help with this," she said.

Professor Milton eyed the item with intense curiosity. "Oh my," she gasped, taking the handle into her hands and carefully inspecting every part. "Where did you find it?"

"A group calling themselves the Servants of Evil claimed it for a dark and unknown master," said Wonder Woman. "Do you know what it is?"

Professor Milton grinned. "It's something I've been tracking for a very long time. One piece of a very dangerous puzzle. It's the handle of an ancient wand that's been missing for thousands of years," she explained.

Professor Milton pulled an antique scroll from a nearby filing cabinet and spread it out across her desk. The scroll showed fearsome monsters ravaging the world, causing chaos and destruction. In the middle of the scene was the wand.

"If the other pieces of the wand are found and assembled, it could destroy the entire planet," Professor Milton said.

Wonder Woman studied the photos carefully. "Do you know where they are?" she pressed.

"The wand's shaft is at the United Nations museum in New York. It's part of an exhibit on the ancient world. The head of the wand is being kept inside a former military base in the mountains of Nevada," Professor Milton explained. "Once they've been collected, give them to me so I can place them in a vault for safekeeping."

"Got it," said Wonder Woman.

"Are you sure you want to go on such a dangerous mission alone, Wonder Woman?" Professor Milton asked. "It will be quite an undertaking, even for a powerful super hero such as yourself."

Before she could answer, Agent Trevor walked into Professor Milton's office.

"I contacted Agent Steve Trevor on my way here," explained Wonder Woman. "He and I have worked together many times before. I trust him with my life."

Steve gave two thumbs up. "And I've always got her back," he said.

"Seems you're prepared for *everything*," Professor Milton remarked. "A true hero."

"She's the best of the best," said Steve. "And I'm not just saying that because she's saved my life many times."

"Come, Agent Trevor. I'll brief you on the mission on the way," Wonder Woman said.

"Wait!" Professor Milton exclaimed, grabbing the jar of chocolate chip cookies on her desk. "Have a cookie before you go. I baked them myself. If you don't, I'll just end up throwing them away."

Steve grabbed a cookie and stuffed it in his mouth. "Tasty," he said. "Thanks!"

Professor Milton waved the jar in front of Wonder Woman. "Are you sure I can't tempt you, Princess? They're *extra* fresh."

Wonder Woman smiled kindly. "No thank you, Professor," she replied. "But I appreciate the offer. We'll be back as soon as possible."

"Good luck out there," said Professor Milton as Wonder Woman and Agent Trevor left her office. Then she turned towards a mirror behind her desk and watched her full-body disguise disappear completely. She smiled at the reflection of the purple-haired sorceress clad in green that stared back at her.

"You're going to need *every* bit of luck you can get!"

# CHAPTER 2

# CHAOS AT THE UNITED NATIONS

Wonder Woman and Agent Trevor boarded the Invisible Jet and took off into the sky. A marvel of Amazonian science, the aircraft used stealth technology to mask it from sight.

"I don't think I'll ever get used to travelling in this crazy jet of yours. Amazons certainly do have a lot of cool stuff," said Steve. "Thanks for inviting me along."

"You and your friends at A.R.G.U.S. have always provided excellent help, which is exactly what this mission requires," Wonder Woman said.

"What's the plan?" asked Steve.

"We're going to track down two pieces of an ancient and powerful wand," the hero explained. She activated a holographic map in the jet's cockpit showing each destination. "The wand's shaft is located at the United Nations. The wand's head is hidden inside a former military base."

"Looks pretty simple to me," said Steve.

"*Looks* can be deceiving. Keep your eyes open and your mind sharp," Wonder Woman said, handing Steve a small box. He eyed it curiously and removed the lid to find a thin rope necklace containing a small pendant.

"Does this turn me invisible? That would be cool," Steve joked. "Though, if I'm being honest, I'd rather be able to fly."

"No superpowers, I'm afraid. The flower inside this Amazonian pendant has been known to protect its wearer," Wonder Woman explained with a smile. "Just think of it as a good luck charm."

"Um, well, I'm not a jewellery guy, but thanks," Steve said. He stuffed the necklace safely into a metal compartment on his utility belt. "So, we're going to grab a couple of old relics, huh? Sounds kind of boring."

"Don't be fooled. We're going up against a dangerous and unpredictable force – dark magic. Be prepared for anything," said Wonder Woman.

"Like I said – *boring!*" Steve exclaimed, putting his feet up onto the jet's dashboard.

A UN delegate pointed at Wonder Woman in anger. His eyes had turned purple. *"You're the one who brought this here!"* he shouted. "Heroes like you cause trouble wherever you go!" "I don't like your tone, mister!" snapped the Secretary-General. Her eyes had turned purple as well. She grabbed a chair and threw it at the angry delegate. Wonder Woman held up her wrists and used her metal bracelets to deflect the oncoming attack.

The chamber erupted into chaos as the delegates began fighting. They tore down flags, toppled desks and threw chairs at one another. One delegate climbed on stage and ripped down the United Nations crest. *"This* is what we *really* think of peace!" he cried.

"Merciful Minerva," Wonder Woman gasped. "Everyone has gone mad."

A delegate sneaked up behind Wonder Woman and smashed a chair across her back. It crumbled to pieces, but the Amazon warrior was unmoved. She took the man by the shoulders and spun him in circles. He became so dizzy, he fell to the ground.

*That bizarre mist has given everyone an angry thirst for violence,* Wonder Woman thought. *This must be the dark magic that Professor Milton warned me about. I've got to stop these people without hurting them.*

A menacing delegate moved in on Wonder Woman from the front. "I bet *you* want *peace*, don't you?" he asked. "Stupid, stupid, stupid."

Another delegate moved in from behind. "All you *heroes* think about is yourself," she said. "How are we supposed to trust people like *you?*"

Secretary-General Acosta looked around the wrecked room, quietly surveying the costly damage.

"Is this the dark magic you spoke of, Wonder Woman?" Acosta asked. "Thank you for what you did to help, but I think it's best if you take what you need and leave."

Wonder Woman understood, but the Secretary-General's words still stung. "Very well," she replied.

Agent Trevor entered the chamber and was shocked by the destruction. "This place is a disaster!" he exclaimed.

Wonder Woman remained silent. She nodded goodbye to Secretary-General Acosta and went to find the piece of the wand.

Steve followed behind. "I cleared the UN museum, so we're good to go," he said.

"The wand's shaft knows we're coming for it," said Wonder Woman.

As they entered the museum, Steve sensed Wonder Woman's frustration. "What happened in there that's got you so upset?"

"There's no time to discuss that right now. Let's complete the mission and be on our way," Wonder Woman said. She spotted the wand's shaft under a glass case in the corner. "There it is."

Steve stared at the simple bar of metal and shrugged. "It doesn't look cursed to me," he said. "Hurry up and grab this thing so we can leave. I've had enough of this mission."

Agent Trevor lifted the top off the case, and Wonder Woman carefully removed the shaft from its display. She gripped it tightly. There was no lightning or thunder. The skies didn't turn black.

"What is that ugly thing?!" Agent Trevor exclaimed.

"A sea creature from Greek mythology," said Wonder Woman. "I read about it as a child. It's an evil beast that will lay waste to the city if given the chance."

"What are *you* going to do?" asked Steve.

Wonder Woman grinned. "I'm going to stop it," she said, handing the wand shaft to Agent Trevor. "Protect this with your life, Steve. I'll be back."

The Amazon warrior launched herself at the beast like a speeding bullet. *I'm not about to let that sea monster come ashore and destroy the city,* she thought. *It's time for me to let loose!*

*SWACK!* Wonder Woman punched the sea creature's snout, knocking it backwards.

The creature stumbled, surprised by the powerful attack. It quickly recovered and charged once again. Wonder Woman gave it another swat to the nose.

"Back off!" she exclaimed. "I won't warn you again."

*ROAR!!!* The angry monster didn't like being told what to do.

The beast swiped its claws wildly, trying to catch Wonder Woman as she zigzagged through the sky. She was too fast for the snarling sea monster.

The angry creature looked around for something else to destroy. It spotted the Queensboro Bridge bustling with cars – the perfect target. As it made its way towards the bridge, Wonder Woman dived into the water. She grabbed one of the beast's many thrashing tentacles.

"Drop it!" Wonder Woman shouted. She grabbed the other end of the vehicle, pulled it from the monster's grip, and returned it safely to the bridge.

*ROAR!!!* The sea creature didn't like having his toys taken away. He bared his claws and began using them to rip apart the bridge. Wonder Woman flew to the very top of the bridge and positioned herself just right.

"This ends now!" she exclaimed, banging her enchanted bracelets together.

*CLANG!* Wonder Woman's colliding bracelets released a powerful shock wave that blasted the beast away from the bridge. The monster struggled to keep its balance, fighting through a dizzy spell.

*The creature is dazed and unaware,* Wonder Woman thought. *It's time to end this once and for all.*

The Amazon warrior flew around the sea monster at super-speed, wrapping her magic lasso around it as tightly as she could. She watched as the beast struggled to free itself, but there was no escape.

Before Wonder Woman could haul the monster away, it disappeared in a burst of light as if it had never existed. But the damage had been done. Innocent lives had been put in danger. The entire episode left Wonder Woman confused.

Joining Steve on the riverbank, Wonder Woman wondered if going up against dark magic was the right idea after all.

"Let's hope that sea creature is the worst thing we meet on our quest," she said.

Steve handed the hero the recovered wand shaft. She studied the simple-looking item carefully.

"We'll have to be extra careful at our next location," Wonder Woman said. "The dark magic that protects these wand pieces isn't going down without a fight."

Steve wasn't sure he wanted to continue on the mission. "What about the people who could've been hurt?" he asked. "You're supposed to be a *hero*, Wonder Woman. You're supposed to keep people *safe*. But your meddling brought the sea monster here. If you hadn't touched that piece of the wand, none of this would have happened."

Steve's sudden shift in perspective confused Wonder Woman. "What are you talking about?" she asked. "According to Professor Milton, if we don't find all of the wand pieces immediately, the whole world might suffer. I can't let that happen."

Steve wasn't convinced.

"That wand is one hundred per cent trouble. You want to find the rest of that stupid thing? Fine. You can do it by yourself," Steve said, swiping the wand shaft from her grasp. "I'm taking this piece back to Professor Milton. Then I'm taking a nice long holiday away from you."

"I don't know what's got into you, Steve," said Wonder Woman. "But fine. You take that piece to Milton. I'll complete the mission alone."

Wonder Woman parted ways with Steve, but his cruel words stayed with her. *If I bring chaos and destruction with me everywhere I go, perhaps I've failed as a hero,* she thought.

It wasn't like Wonder Woman to doubt herself, but maybe Steve was right. Maybe she wasn't the champion of peace she thought she was.

Echidna opened her mouth and shot a stream of poisonous venom in Wonder Woman's direction. The Amazon warrior swiftly raised her shield, blocking the attack. The warm venom sizzled as it splashed against Wonder Woman's protective armour.

"How about a taste of your own vile medicine?" Wonder Woman asked. She threw the venom-covered shield towards Echidna, striking the serpentine monster in the face.

**SCREECH!**

Echidna didn't like that one bit. She slapped her snake tail on the cavern floor repeatedly. Each blow shook the mountain.

Time was running out. Wonder Woman had to retrieve her prize. As if reading her mind, Echidna reached into the crate and grabbed the head of the wand. Wrestling it from her grasp wasn't going to be easy.

"You'll never win, Amazon," taunted the mysterious voice. "You're far too weak. You're much too feeble. Give up now or face embarrassment later."

At last, Wonder Woman realized exactly who the voice belonged to.

*Circe!* she thought. *It all makes sense now. Circe is the one who cursed the wand with dark magic in the first place. That ancient witch is up to something. I need to grab the final piece of the wand before it falls into her hands.*

**SCREECH!**

Echidna lunged towards Wonder Woman. The hero ducked and rolled to avoid her.

"Our battle is at an end, monster!" Wonder Woman exclaimed. She threw her golden lasso around the giant snake-woman and held on tight.

"Where am I?" Steve wondered aloud. "What happened to me?"

"Awww. He doesn't *remember*. That's probably for the best. You betrayed your friend, *Steve*," Circe said. "You planted seeds of doubt in her mind and made her feel like a failure. *You* helped destroy Wonder Woman."

Steve couldn't believe what he was hearing. "Is Circe right, Wonder Woman?" he asked. "Is it my fault we're in this mess?"

"Circe poisoned your mind. You weren't in control of yourself," Wonder Woman explained. She directed her growing anger towards Circe. "No more lies and deception, witch. Tell me what you want."

"World domination in the long term. In the short term, I want your *weapons* and *armour*. I want you to bow before me in total surrender," Circe revealed. "How about it?"

"Never!" Wonder Woman barked.

"Then you leave me no choice," Circe said. She swirled the wand through the air and produced a new creature of myth. The enormous beast had red eyes, dark grey skin and a handful of tentacles. A pair of scaly wings burst from its back. "This is Echidna's husband, Typhon, the Father of Monsters," she said. "Be nice and say hello, Typhon."

**ROAR!!!**

Typhon's cry shattered all of the glass display cases inside the museum.

"Isn't he wonderful?" asked Circe. "Show Wonder Woman how you attack, boy."

Typhon smashed through the museum wall, crashing onto the street outside. He grabbed a parked car, picked it up and threw it into the air like a toy.

*I have to act fast,* Wonder Woman thought.

The Amazon raced to the scene, swiftly catching the vehicle before it fell to the ground. Innocent bystanders ran for their lives as Typhon continued his rampage.

Wonder Woman charged the monster, striking him in the face with her shield. At the same moment, a fleet of A.R.G.U.S. troopers arrived on the scene. They'd been sent to stop Typhon before he destroyed Washington DC.

"Go away, swine!" Circe shouted. With a wave of her wand, she turned all of the A.R.G.U.S. troopers into squealing piglets. "That's *much* better."

Wonder Woman raised her sword to deliver the final blow. But before she could strike, Typhon suddenly disappeared.

Wonder Woman slowly made her way towards Circe. As she got closer, the villainess began to lose her balance. Circe waved her wand, but it only produced a small spark.

"What's going on here?" the villain asked. "My magic is fading."

Wonder Woman showed off Steve's pendant. "This contains an ancient flowering herb called Moly," she explained. "In modern times, it's been used for good luck. But it's original purpose was . . ."

"To disrupt my power," Circe growled. "Get it away from me!" She pointed her wand at Wonder Woman, but the Amazon warrior kicked it out of her hand before she could use it.

"No!" Circe exclaimed. She chased the wand, scrambling to grab her most prized possession as it rolled away.

# CIRCE

**BASE:**
Aeaea

**SPECIES:**
Olympian

**OCCUPATION:**
Sorceress

**HEIGHT:**
1.8 metres

**WEIGHT:**
66 kilograms

**EYES:**
Blue

**HAIR:**
Purple

**POWERS/ABILITIES:**
Nearly limitless magical power, including the power to transform mortal beings into animals. She also has the power to project her voice, image and energy bolts over long distances.

## BIOGRAPHY:

Circe is an ancient sorceress who has a mischievous spirit and a flair for the dramatic. The villain practises the art of dark magic, though she's far from perfect at using it. Her magical abilities include changing people into animals, projecting her voice, firing magical energy blasts and teleporting between dimensions. Over the millennia, Circe has taken many different forms in order to trick people into doing her bidding. One never knows where she might pop up next.

- Circe hates Wonder Woman and everything she stands for. She has spent a large amount of time plotting against the Amazon Princess and believes it's the hero's fault she has yet to become a villainous powerhouse.

- Circe loves nothing more than to humiliate others. That may be why animal transformation is one of her magical specialities. More often than not, those who cross her find themselves turned into pigs!

- Circe may have magic on her side, but Wonder Woman has a little magic of her own. The Amazon warrior's silver bracelets are the perfect defence against Circe's sorcery. They allow Wonder Woman to block magic, preventing damage and transformation.

# DISCUSSION QUESTIONS

**1.** Wonder Woman trusts Steve because he's one of her closest friends. Who is a friend you trust? What are some positive qualities that make him or her trustworthy?

**2.** Wonder Woman gives Steve the pendant as a good luck charm. Do you believe in good luck charms? Explain why or why not.

**3.** Circe used dark magic to make Wonder Woman doubt herself. Describe a time when you doubted your abilities. Explain how you overcame your feelings of uncertainty.

# WRITING PROMPTS

1. Imagine you had a magic wand like Circe's. What would you do with it? Write a short story about your adventures with your magic wand.

2. Circe turned Steve into a half-human, half-animal Bestiamorph. Draw a picture of what you think Steve looked like in this monstrous form and label his most interesting features.

3. At the end of the story, Wonder Woman promises to take Circe to the island of Themyscira to face Amazonian justice. Write a new chapter that shows what happens when they get there. Does Circe go to prison or does she escape? You decide!

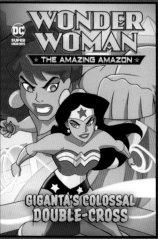